KU-073-132

EGMONT

We bring stories to life

First published in Great Britain in 2007 by Dean,
an imprint of Egmont UK Limited
239 Kensington High Street, London W8 6SA

Thomas the Tank Engine & Friends™

A BRITT ALLCROFT COMPANY PRODUCTION

Based on The Railway Series by The Reverend W Awdry
Photographs © 2007 Gullane (Thomas) LLC. A HIT Entertainment Company

Thomas the Tank Engine & Friends and Thomas & Friends are trademarks of Gullane (Thomas) Limited.
Thomas the Tank Engine & Friends and Design is Reg. US. Pat. & Tm. Off.

ISBN 978 0 6035 6260 0
1 3 5 7 9 10 8 6 4 2
Printed in Singapore

All rights reserved. No part of this publication may be reproduced, stored in a retrieval system,
or transmitted, in any form or by any means, electronic, mechanical, photocopying, recording or
otherwise, without the prior permission of the publisher and copyright owner.

Thomas and the Ghost Engine

The Thomas TV Series

It was Halloween on the Island of Sodor. The Fat Controller was going to have fireworks, and all the engines were very excited.

Edward was telling the engines spooky stories while they waited for the fireworks to start.

"They say that on Halloween, a ghost engine returns to the Smelter's Yard, looking for his lost whistle!" said Edward.

"Spooky!" said the other engines.

Just then, The Fat Controller came into the shed.

"Thomas, Percy and Duck, I have a special job for you," said The Fat Controller. "I want you to collect some scrap from the Smelter's Yard tonight."

"On Halloween?" asked Percy, feeling scared.

"Don't worry, Percy," smiled The Fat Controller. "You won't miss the fireworks!"

"Percy isn't worried about missing the fireworks," teased Thomas. "He's a scaredy engine!"

"I am not!" cried Percy. But he *was* a bit scared!

Percy, Duck and Thomas steamed off to the Smelter's Yard. Thomas teased him all the way there.

When they arrived at the yard, all Percy could think about was the ghost engine.

"What's that up there?" said Thomas. "Is it a ghost?"

"It's just a piece of scrap . . . isn't it?" said Percy, nervously.

Thomas giggled. He was having fun teasing Percy.

"Careful the ghost engine doesn't get you!" Thomas said to Percy, as they did their work.

"There are no such things as ghosts!" snapped Percy, though he wasn't feeling too sure.

Duck felt sorry for Percy.

"Nobody's brave all the time," he said.

Soon the job was nearly finished.

"Well done," said the Yard Manager. "I just need one engine to stay and finish up."

Duck wanted to pay Thomas back for teasing Percy. "I'm sure Thomas wouldn't mind staying," said Duck.

"Of course not," puffed Thomas, proudly. "I'm not a scaredy engine!"

So Duck and Percy left Thomas all alone.

As soon as Thomas was by himself, he started to feel scared. The Smelter's Yard was very spooky.

"There are no such things as ghosts!" he said to himself. But he couldn't stop looking out for them.

Thomas was so busy searching for ghosts, he didn't look where he was going! He ran into something that brushed against his face.

"Ghost fingers!" cried Thomas.

Thomas was too scared to see that the ghost fingers were just some old chains!

"Help! Something's got me!" shouted Thomas. "It's the ghost engine!"

And he raced away as fast as his wheels could carry him!

Thomas steamed along the track. "The ghost engine is after me!" he cried.

Back at the sheds, the other engines were waiting for the fireworks to start.

"It was naughty of Thomas to tease you, Percy," said Duck.

"He was only playing," said Percy, kindly. "I hope he hurries up. I don't want him to be late for the fireworks!"

Just then, Thomas rushed past them at top speed!

"The ghost engine is after me!" wailed Thomas.

Duck laughed and laughed.

"Thomas isn't as brave as he makes out," chuckled Duck.

The fireworks were about to start, but Thomas still had not arrived.

"Where's Thomas?" Percy asked. "He'll miss all the fun!"

"It would serve him right after all his teasing," said Duck.

But Percy was worried. He went to look for his friend.

Thomas was all alone in the shed.

"Are you all right, Thomas?" asked Percy.

"Yes, and I'm sorry I teased you," said Thomas. He felt guilty. "Duck was right. We all feel scared sometimes."

"And we all have to say sorry sometimes," smiled Percy. "Come on, Thomas, we can watch the fireworks just as well from here!"

And so they did!